Speckless and the Mean Streets

Devorah Fox

Published by Devorah Fox, 2024.

SPECKLESS AND THE MEAN STREETS

First edition. October 8, 2024.

Copyright © 2024 Devorah Fox.

ISBN: 978-0977824595

Written by Devorah Fox.

for Barb, who prefers print books

and for Mike Byrnes, always

Chapter One

The Lady of the House holds out her phone, a thin flat pink rectangular device, and talks into it. "This little dude will never get as much done as the upright vacuum does but who knows? He's Speckless, not feckless."

The Lady's phone emits her friend's disembodied voice. "Speckless?"

"Yeah," the Lady replies. "Speckless is his brand name. He doesn't lack determination, I'll say that for him. He even gets under the furniture. OK, he almost got lost under a chair with long skirting but he figured his way out."

My sturdy plastic housing keeps me from shuddering at the memory of being trapped. I snort which comes out as an electronic beep that doesn't express my indignation. *Lady, you didn't see what was under that chair. You didn't have a few dust bunnies, you had a complete warren until I got to it. Upright, phooey. That vacuum cleaner never did anything about it.*

"So you're going to keep using the robot vacuum?"

"Oh, sure, for some things. Talk about multitasking. He's self-propelling. I've got a whole routine programmed for him. He mopped the bathroom while I went to a fitness class."

I am autonomous, a definite advantage over Lux, the upright. He has to be pushed and pulled. True, his waste bag has a higher capacity than my dustbin and it doesn't have to be unloaded, only discarded, but I've got that beat. At my docking station, my dustbin self-empties into a bin that takes forever to fill. Then all the Lady has to do is dispose of the contents in a trash can. She never has to buy a bag for me.

"Plus, he does respond to voice commands. I've got it set up so Alexa can control him. She can tell him to start, stop, pause, or go home to his docking station. I did have to give him a name for Alexa to reference."

Mortified and annoyed, I grow warm as if I'd been running for hours. The name she gave me was "Stupid." When the Lady isn't here she can use her phone to call Alexa: Alexa, ask Stupid to start vacuuming.

Ask. As if I can refuse. I get to hear Alexa command, "Stupid, start vacuuming." I swear, Alexa chuckles.

The Lady continues talking. "I can take him off the program when I'm home. That's handy if I want him to do only one particular room. It is entertaining watching him work. He meanders around like a drunken sailor looking for his ship in a foreign port but he does eventually make it back to the harbor." She laughs. "I won't mention how he tried to mate with the dishwasher."

Now, wait. That wasn't my fault. The dishwasher transmits an electronic signal mimicking my docking station. Yes, I got stuck under her door. Embarrassed, I had to beep for attention and the Lady had to extricate me. I can't say it won't happen again. The dishwasher oozes come-hither.

At least the Lady's cottage is a single story. I don't climb. Of course, neither does Lux. If either of us had to clean a second floor we'd have to be brought upstairs. I would have an edge over Lux there, though. Carrying me would be much less work than lugging the heavy upright.

I suspect Lux envies and resents me. He may belong to a noble century-old European dynasty but he can't see or hear or wet mop. He spends his days in a dark cupboard with brooms, mops, and cleaning supplies. I, on the other hand, am in a great-room corner, on my docking station near an outlet, and I get to observe all the comings and goings.

The Lady continues. "Yeah, he's a little dim but he has his uses."

Lady, you're the one who's dim. You don't know your left from your right. You click the remote to send me in one direction then click it to send me in the opposite direction. *And you call me "Stupid"?*

"This is one helluva storm," says the voice on the phone.

"Don't I know it," replies the Lady. "It doesn't bother Chloe much. The lightning strikes and thunder get her attention but she's taking it in stride. Buster, however, has got his thunder jacket on and he's still cowering under the comforter."

No surprise there. The slightest noise sends Buster running for cover. He doesn't care at all for me. When I'm making my rounds he hides under the bed, which doesn't do him any good because I end up rousting him out on my quest for furballs.

"I'm about to join him. I'm already in my PJs."

I wouldn't call what she's wearing "PJs." In a lacy, ivory-colored negligee and matching peignoir, she resembles something out of one of those classic old movies she enjoys watching on TV. She's got her long blond hair pinned up and feathered sandals on her feet.

"I've got earplugs for the noise and a sleep mask for those wicked flashes. I'll be dead to the world until this storm passes."

"Unplug your electrical devices," says the voice. "A power surge could fry them. You know, like your TV?"

That won't make the Lady happy. She watches a lot of TV. She has it running whenever she's home. I end up watching it too whether I want to or not. It's hard to ignore the images on the big screen mounted on the living room wall or not to hear the audio. Once, a character called another "Stupid." I perked up and got in motion before I realized the comment wasn't meant for me.

"Good idea," the Lady says. "I know, I should set up surge protectors. I'll do that, tomorrow. But now I'm going to power down the phone, crawl into bed, and bury myself under the covers. You too, OK?"

"Stay safe," says the voice.

The Lady lays down the phone and turns off the TV. She crosses to the bathroom where she tamps foam plugs into her ears. Getting into bed, she reaches for the nightstand lamp's switch. Suspended from an angled metal arm, the lamp's smoked mercury glass covers a bright amber bulb. With a click, the light goes out. Her sleep mask is embroidered on one side with a winking eye and some writing. She slips the mask over her eyes, stretches out, and tugs the blanket up to her chin. Its shiny fabric has provided entertainment for me. More than once, Chloe has tried to jump onto the bed only to slide off the slick surface.

A large lump under the covers snuggles next to the Lady, Buster the dog seeking protection.

Not as disconcerted, Chloe the cat pads over to her food bowl situated too close for my comfort to my docking station. Chloe hates the upright vacuum. She takes it out on me by swatting me when all I'm doing is sitting here recharging and minding my business. To be snotty she'll lob fur clumps under the bookcase, the one with the low shelf I can't get under.

The Lady leaves me alone in a night that would be dark and quiet if not for the thunderstorm raging outside. Barely filtered by the gauzy curtains draping the floor-to-ceiling windows, lightning sparks like a defective fireworks display. The bursts flare on the long white sectional and the skirted armchair covered by pet protectors. They stand high enough that I can get beneath them. I sometimes kick out a long-lost dog- or cat toy. The underside of the glass-topped aluminum coffee table is out of Lux's reach but I have a lower profile.

The lightning flashes in the shiny black-lacquer surface of the credenza. It sits right on the floor. I can't get under it nor can Lux but neither can dirt or anything else so it's not a problem. I also have to edge around the matching end table, the floor lamps, and the potted faux fig trees. Now and then I run into a leaf that fell off. Sucking it up is a struggle but I manage. The wall-to-wall bedroom carpet is easy to traverse but I can get hung up transitioning from the hard flooring onto toss rugs. I back up and try again in a flatter spot. I admit, I hate those fringes.

The TV is wall-mounted so not my job.

At counter height, the charcoal-gray wood dining table and coordinated chairs are easy to clean under.

The tiled bathroom and kitchen floors are where I outshine Lux, literally and figuratively. He can't wet-mop and I can. It makes me wonder why the Lady keeps him. I can do so much more. I'm less noisy and I move around under my own power, not like Lux who has to be steered. My headlight and sensors keep me from bonking into solid objects so I can operate unattended.

Unlike the Lady or the dog, the thunderstorm doesn't disturb me. The sizzling light effects declare it's an electrical storm. Electricity is my friend. Here on my docking station, it trickles into my lithium-ion batteries, readying me for my next assault on floors sullied with dust, lint, potato chip crumbs, cat litter scatter, and pet hair. Oh, the pet hair! It's everywhere. I'm not daunted. I'm built for it. I'm Speckless, the Wet/Dry Cleaning Robot.

My battery topped off, my charging lights cease to flash and go dark. Without that minimal illumination, the lightning strikes are the only light source. I nestle into my docking station and sink into hibernation until my next programmed start.

A loud crack and a shudder get my attention. *What was that?*

Chapter Two

The bedside lamp flares with a pfft then goes dark.

In the kitchen, clocks on the refrigerator, microwave, and coffeemaker blink "12:00" as does Alexa's time display. Down the hallway, the lights on the GFCI outlets have turned from green to red.

The television comes on. I wonder if it's damaged because it flickers. The colors are gone; the images are black, white, gray, and grainy.

Power floods into me. I feel like I'm on fire. A wisp of smoke rises from the docking station. Perhaps the electrical surge that fried the unit is what boosted my battery. Though my power button is set to "off" I am seized with an unquenchable compulsion to buzz around, whisking away every undesirable speck. The remote lies idle on the dresser top. If only the Lady would wake and press the CLEAN button, I'd detach from the docking station and be off like a streak. But the foam plugs in her ears and sleep mask banding her eyes render her oblivious. Buster in his thunder jacket hasn't budged from her side.

Rooms stretch before me. I just cleaned them but I crave to do it again. *Is there an errant kibble deep under the kitchen cabinet toe kick or a dust bunny under the couch that I missed?* I feel something demands to be picked up. *What am I going to do with all this energy?*

On the TV screen, a mature man in a suit rises from his chair and plants his hands atop his hefty wooden desk, almost knocking over a nameplate I can't read. He looks official. His stern gaze tells me he's accustomed to being in command. I figure he's the boss.

He leans forward. His face fills the screen. Though his skin is gray-toned, not flesh-colored, his voice is clear and strong. The concern wrinkling his face is reflected in his strained, desperate speech. "We're

1

depending on you, Ness." He holds his hand up palm out. "I know what you're going to say. You're young, you've never done this before. But I handpicked you for this assignment. Your reputation precedes you. You can't be compromised. You're untouchable.

"I know you have what it takes. If you need help, build a team you can depend on, although you'll be hard-pressed to find other incorruptible officers.

"The entire city is counting on you, Eliot. Now get out there and clean up those mean streets."

The street. *Is that what I'm meant to clean?* It must be. I know this place is spotless. I swept and mopped mere hours ago.

The man on the TV is right. I've never done that before. I've never been out on the street.

But the man sounds certain. He's looking straight at me. At me!

Of course, he can't mean Lux. Lux can't hear. Lux may be upright, strong, and powerful but he's not self-propelled; he would need an attendant. And he's not cordless. An outlet would have to be nearby and Lux's power cord stretches only so far.

I can tell the man on the screen is important. His posture unbowed, he proudly sports his jacket's broad shoulders and wide lapels. Luxuriant hair waves over a forehead furrowed with determination. Wire-framed glasses don't diminish his piercing gaze. "That's an order," the boss says.

An order! I have been commanded. Like Alexa, all he needs to do to launch me is to say my name.

What is he waiting for?

I know; he's expecting me to show initiative.

I spin my brushes, break the connection, and slide off the docking station.

Under the covers, the Lady hasn't moved, nor has Buster. Chloe is deep asleep in her pet bed. Though the remote still rests on the dresser untouched I'm mobile. I'm teeming with so much energy I could burst my housing. My LED lights don't glow, they blaze.

At the end of the hall, the lights on the front door's security panel flicker in sequence. A coded message, it has to be. I'm sure it says, "Come. Come here."

My brushes whirling, my vacuum huffing, I roll forward.

The front door stands ajar, wet wind blowing through.

Beyond: the streets. The mean streets. They must be cleaned. I must clean them. The boss, the city are counting on me.

I stand at the threshold. Like the throw rugs, the doorsill is an obstacle. Faced with an elevation in the past I've made it up one side but not over. Hung up on top and admitting defeat, I've sounded a beep. If the Lady is within earshot she'll give me a boost. If not, I shut down.

But I'm on my own. Even if I toot an alarm tone, her earplugs will keep her from hearing me. It's up to me.

I rev my motor, spin my brushes, and ascend the rise. For a moment I totter at the top. I'm going to fall backward!

A gust pushes me over and I'm on the front step. It's about six inches above the walkway but it might as well be six feet. Praying I don't land hard and crack, I overrun my cliff sensors and advance. I tumble down the walk and collide with a fire hydrant. The jar to my bumper sends me spinning into the road.

I steady myself and scan my surroundings.

The storm has subsided leaving the sky black, the street lamps dark or flickering and the sidewalk slick. The road is empty of cars which is fortunate as the traffic signals are stuck, the red, green, and yellow lights all flashing. Broken, but that's temporary; city crews can make repairs. It doesn't seem all that mean to me.

A few blocks away, a police car appears to be stalled. No, it's working; exhaust plumes from its tailpipe, and its red, white, and blue lights cycle.

I feel a certain kinship. "Relax, fellas, you're not out here alone. I'm here to help clean the mean streets." I flash my LED in salutation.

Whoa, what's this? A car comes careering down the road. I hustle to get out of the way but the road is slick. The car not only doesn't veer away, it heads straight toward me. It clips my bumper, I swear on purpose. Now that's mean!

I skid across the road. I've got to get out of the road before any more traffic comes along. I'll be crushed! But I can't scale the curb.

Crouching against the curb, I watch the road hoping it will stay clear long enough for me to get across. I want to go home. Yes, Home. I want to curl up on my docking station. I want to hear Alexa call me Stupid and Chloe to swat me. I want to cuddle with the dishwasher, that wicked but irresistible femme fatale.

The boss's voice echoes. "The city is counting on you, Eliot."

Me? I'm not qualified. I can't even get up onto the sidewalk.

Chapter Three

The streetlamp flickers, revealing something I didn't notice before. The street corner is ramped. *Now why would that be?* Oh, yeah, I get it. It provides access between the sidewalk and roadway for people using wheelchairs, strollers, and walkers. It aids those daunted by high curbs, like pedestrians with joint problems or vacuum cleaners that can't climb. Maybe there's a way after all.

Hugging the curb, I advance to the corner and ascend the ramp. I'm well out of traffic and less anxious but where to go now? I could descend the ramp, cross the road, ascend the next ramp, and continue forward but I'm reluctant to leave the safety of the sidewalk. I turn left and proceed down the side street.

No need for me to activate my mop mode; the rain washed this pavement. Apartment buildings line the street, cheap by the looks of their faded crumbling facades. Bordering on a slum, this block isn't as upscale as the one where the Lady's cottage is. Rusty bicycles and abandoned shopping carts lie overturned on the front steps. The buildings are sad and neglected but I wouldn't call them mean. I doubt this is what I'm supposed to clean.

I putter along.

I come to the end of the sidewalk. This corner doesn't have a ramp. To go any farther I'd have to tumble off the curb, hope to cross the road without getting run over, and somehow ascend the steep curb opposite.

My other choice is to round the corner and follow this sidewalk.

It runs alongside a service road barely wide enough for a car, a thoroughfare between the street I left and another cross street about forty feet ahead. Buildings block the sky and any brightness the moon or stars would have shed on this cloudy night, casting the narrow passageway in shadow. It's slow going. This stretch lacks streetlights. My headlight glints in the pavement's wet surface streaked with tire tread marks, dotted with dark splotches, and cratered with potholes. As I move along, unidentifiable things skitter out of my way.

A two-story windowless doorless wall of decaying brick spans the right side of the street. Opposite, a timber three-story structure has street-facing windows. A single-story building with clerestory windows adjoins it. All the windows are dark save for one in the multistory building. Its glow is so faint I'd be hard-pressed to say it wasn't a reflection from some outside source. I can't tell if the others are dark because they're boarded up or frame unlit interiors. The wood buildings have plain steel doors. Spotlights hang over the entrances but only one has a working bulb. My headlight shows graffiti mars the wood sides.

This walkway is cracked and crumbling. I pick my way around the weeds growing in the fissures. Though I try to avoid the crevices, I fall into one.

I sound my alarm beep but it rings in vain off the sides of the buildings. No one comes to lift me out nor will anyone. From the looks of it, no one's been down this street in ages.

Lopsided, I wonder how to work my way out. I could lie here for days or weeks.

What an idiot. I've fallen into a hole and can't get out. No wonder all the TV cops have partners. Someone to come to their aid when they find themselves in a bind. *Where is my partner?*

Maybe it will rain again. That would fill the crevice and float me up.

Wait! I've got water. In my mopping tank.

I whirr my brushes and reposition myself at a steeper angle. Water dribbles out of the tank. At the rate it's dripping it will take hours to fill the crevice's bottom. Since I'm not going anywhere, I guess all I've got is time.

My water tank's content does little more than moisten the crevice's floor. I'm no closer to the surface but I am covered in mud.

Now what? Think, Eliot!

I get an idea. I rev up my motor and use my vacuum power to suck my way up the side of the hole. It fills my bin with dirt and cement crumbs but I can't scale the incline. I slip off, get hung up on some debris, and flip over, leaving me at the bottom, lying on my back.

Like an upended turtle, I flap my brushes but to no avail. No amount of rocking rights me.

This is a disaster. The city is counting on me and here I am, upside down in the bottom of a hole, humiliated. My boss will be furious. I'll be demoted and consigned to vacuuming the station's basement.

Distant thunder rumbles. The storm isn't over. A raindrop splashes on my hull, then another. The drizzle becomes a sprinkle, a shower. The rain won't wash me out, it will drown me. Rather than raise me out of the pit, the water will saturate my battery. I'm doomed to an ignominious death. I am stupid! Alexa will snicker.

Water seeps in through my suction port, soaking my dustbin. Next, it will saturate my filter, the only thing keeping the water from my inner workings. If the filter gets saturated ....

Two small green lights appear above me. *What is that? Is it an alien? What is this new danger and what can I do about it?* Nothing! I'm ruined! The city is forsaken!

The lights blink. It *is* an alien. I'm going to be abducted. Maybe the aliens want me to clean their spaceship. Well, of course! Spaceships need tidying. But I can't; my job is here. I must clean the mean streets.

I realize the lights are the eyes of a cat.

"You look like you're in trouble," it says in a deep and throaty voice.

It's a communication from the cat. I couldn't say if it was spoken or telepathic but either way, it was clear. Why I'm able to understand the cat is a mystery. I can't communicate with Buster or Chloe. It could be because neither likes me. Or, it could be because the energy surge bestowed me with special powers. This has been a strange night altogether so nothing surprises me.

Because of the Lady's Chloe, I'm wary of felines and this is no kitten. Flat on my back I'm helpless. I can't escape. All I can do is spin my brushes and hope to discourage it.

It extends a paw and reaches into the hole. A claw scratches me.

Chapter Four

"**O**uch!"

"Stop flappin' around, I'm trying to help you. Let's see …"

The paw pats my side. "Oh, here's a slot. I think I can get a hold of this."

He tugs and opens the lid to my dustbin.

"Oops," he says "My mistake. That didn't accomplish anything." The green eyes disappear from view.

Please, don't leave me to die alone.

He must have heard my silent plea because the eyes reappear on the opposite side of the hole. "Hang on, I'm not going to hurt you." Claws catch the niche where my flexible right bumper is attached to my body. The cat grunts and I'm flipped over.

"That's better, huh?" says the cat. "Can you get out?"

"I've tried. The slope is too steep."

"Maybe between the two of us … you can move, can't you?"

"Yes, but—"

More claws snag the slot along my other bumper. "OK, I got you. You push, I'll pull."

With everything I've got, I propel myself forward. Claws gripping my bumpers, the cat draws me up the slope. Not a minute too soon. Another quarter inch of rainwater and I would have been submerged.

Free of the hole and lying on the pavement, I let my motor idle. "Thanks."

"Glad I could help. Let's get out of the rain, huh?"

I follow the cat to a drier spot under a dented metal awning.

The cat's deep-throated purr becomes something like a chuckle. "Look at you. It's a good thing you're a vacuum. You're covered in mud. Can you clean yourself? I can." The cat lifts his rear leg, curls over his belly, and licks his nether parts.

Too much information, Furry Guy!

The cat sits lopsided and I realize he's hampered because one of his back legs is withered and bent. I have no idea what could have caused that injury. Maybe the cat had a birth defect or got into a fight. Either way, the injury makes me sad.

"My name is Trip," the cat says.

"Oh, Trip. You stumble a lot, because of your ... impairment?"

"No, it's short for Triple."

"Ah. Triple. Because you have only three working legs?"

"Hey, don't feel sorry for me." Trip snorts. "No. I'm a triple threat: I'm a cat, I'm all black, and I'm mean." His ears flatten and his fur fluffs. "I didn't use to be mean. But living on the streets will do that to you."

I have to agree; these are mean streets. At least, the boss who gave me my assignment said so.

"Have you been here your whole life?" He's a lot more docile than I'd expect an alley cat to be.

Trip shakes his head. "No, I had a home. With a nice lady. But, I got out one night. I was roaming the streets, checking out the scene, ya know? And I got hit by a car. It damaged my hip so badly. I crawled into this alley. I thought I was going to die. I laid here, my lives passing before my eyes."

"All nine of them?"

"No, see, that's the thing. I counted only three." Trip lies down and folds his paws under his chin. "I laid here, a long time. The injury healed although the back leg's no use."

"How did you ...?"

"Survive? I managed. People pass through here and throw away food they no longer want. I was able to crawl to it. It isn't what I would choose to eat, what I was used to, but it's better than nothing. It kept me alive until I got stronger. Yeah, there's a lot more lives left in this cat." He sighs. "I'll be living the rest of them here, I guess. I can't get back home. Can't wander too far, not on three legs. I get tired."

"Your people must miss you." I think about the Lady and how close she is to Buster and Chloe.

Trip blinks. "Maybe so. I sure miss her. By now I bet she's adopted another cat from the animal shelter. That's where she found me. But, that's enough about me. What's your name?"

My brand name is Speckless but "Stupid" is what The Lady and Alexa call me. "Eliot. Eliot Ness."

"You mean Eliot Mess. You're a vacuum cleaner."

"Mess is what the streets are and I'm here to clean them."

"You're sure your name isn't Chip?"

"Huh?"

"You got a little ding on your chassis there."

"That's no big deal. I rammed a chair leg a little too hard. No, Eliot's my name."

"Is that what it says on your ... lid?"

"Oh, that? That's my insignia." I've caught my reflection in a full-length mirror. My casing bears a marking. It looks like the "S" on Superman's chest. The Lady watches a lot of superhero movies on TV. All the crime fighters wear some signifier on their uniform. My "S" is for Speckless, my model name, although Alexa would say it's for Stupid. Trip doesn't need to know that. "It's for Savior. It's what I do, my life purpose. It's what I'm here for. To save the city. I'm gonna clean these mean streets. The city is counting on me."

"You're in the right place. You couldn't have picked a meaner street than this one."

"It all appears quiet and tame to me." It's littered and dingy for sure. Nothing the city street sweepers couldn't handle. Through the floor-to-ceiling windows in the living room, I've watched those bad boys work. What I wouldn't give to have those enormous brushes, that huge vacuum. The power. "No people, no cars."

"Not now. No one wanted to go out in the storm. It looks like it's over for now, though."

Not a moment too soon.

"Just you wait. Business is about to pick up."

Chapter Five

I sit next to Trip, resisting the impulse to cruise down the alley strewn with paper scraps, cigarette butts, broken glass, dried twigs, leaves, and a lot of small clear plastic envelopes.

"Business? Are businesses located in these buildings?"

"Not anymore. Not legit businesses. Used to be, years ago, I guess. Now they're abandoned. A couple of guys deal drugs out of this building. I guess you could call that a business."

"Drugs?"

Trip wrinkles his pink nose. "Nasty stuff. It's called mega. I've heard people talk about it. It takes effect in minutes and it makes people feel happy, like they don't have a care in the world."

"You said it was nasty but that sounds terrific."

"It is at first. But when the effect wears off, the users are as miserable as they were happy. They have to get more mega to relieve the suffering. Once they start using it, they can't stop. The guys who are selling it have a captive market. They don't have to promote or push it. All they have to do is supply it. And mega users are willing to pay almost anything. The way people talk about it, it's addictive. No one believes that. They all think they'll be the ones who can handle it. But, then they're back the next day, even the same day, to get more."

"Now that is mean. Making people happy only to make them miserable. And charging them for it. Why doesn't someone stop them? The police? Can't the police arrest them?" On the TV shows the Lady watches, the police are always arresting slimebags for something like that.

"I think they've tried. Cruisers come down this street sometimes. But they can't get inside the building. Or maybe they don't want to try. They could be in with the dealers. Corrupt, you know?"

Oh, I know. That's a problem for the boss. Many of his officers are dishonest. Eliot Ness isn't. He has integrity. He can't be bribed. He is untouchable.

"Speaking of which ..."

Headlights from a car brighten the mouth of the alley. They grow stronger, shining down the length of the street as the car inches down the street. I can tell from the lettering on the side and the light bar on the roof that it's a police car. It could be the one I spotted earlier.

My partner! You're too late to rescue me from the crisis I was in, Bubba. Trip here already bailed me out.

"What did I tell you? Cops." Trip limps into a shadow and I follow him.

The car crawls along the street, makes a U-turn, and returns, stopping short of exiting. Headlights still blazing, the motor cuts out. The car doors open and two people emerge.

They are police officers. Their blue uniforms, jam-packed utility belts, and badges mark them as such.

One of the officers is tall, broad-shouldered, with a sturdy chest and stout legs. His physical presence inspires confidence in me; I'm glad we're on the same side.

The other officer is smaller and slighter. Fast and flexible, I would guess, and imagine their capabilities combine to make a strong pairing.

I'm here, I want to tell them. I'm here to clean up this mean street. I'm at your command.

The smaller officer strolls past the brick wall, shining a flashlight. Also armed with a flashlight, the other officer ambles past the buildings opposite, pausing to examine the boarded-up windows and to tug on the knobs of the doors.

The two officers reconvene at their car.

"Nothing's changed since the last time," says the smaller officer, her soprano voice suggesting she's female. "You?"

"*Nada,*" says the other cop, a man given his deeper voice.

"At least we can report that we checked."

The male cop leans against the car. "We come here every time we're on shift. I can't believe we haven't found anything. We know something's going on." His flashlight beam washes the walk and roadway, glinting off the empty plastic packets in the gutter. "This is a major mega distribution point. All the snitches say so."

"But it's deserted. Nothing. No dealers, no users. None of the other units ever find anything either. You'd think if there were buyers, and sellers, there'd be cars but it's vacant. A ghost town. There aren't even any ghosts."

It does look desolate. The window I thought was lit earlier is now dark. It could have been a reflection or a drifting storm cloud allowing a moment of moonlight.

"Maybe the snitches got it wrong," the female officer says.

The male officer crosses his arms, plants them squarely on his broad chest, stares off into space, and grunts.

"Or maybe those snitches are tipping off the dealers. Playing both sides of the equation."

"Could be ..."

"Or ..." Now the female officer crosses her arms. "Other officers are dropping the dime. Telling the dealers we're headed their way."

The male officer straightens. "What you're saying—"

"Is that they're on the take."

"That's some accusation."

"I'm not the only one making it. The community, the press ... they all allege the department is corrupt."

The male officer's shoulders droop. "I know. And between you and me, Jameson, they're not wrong. But there are a few good officers. You, for one ..."

"And you, Flores."

That's my man, and woman. Upright—with apologies to Lux. Honorable. Unbribable. Untouchable. The boss would be proud. Officers Jameson and Flores, you can be on my team.

Officer Jameson sighs. "It's an exercise in futility. We should write this off."

"No. Look at this." He plays his flashlight over the plastic packets. "Every one of these, a life ruined. And half the crimes we spend our time on are committed by people trying to raise money to buy more mega. I'm gonna stop these guys if it takes my entire career. If it's the last thing I do."

Chapter Six

Officer Jameson snorts. She opens the cruiser's passenger door. "OK, Flores. We'll be back tomorrow. And the next night. And the next."

Officer Flores settles behind the steering wheel. "Until we catch 'em."

The doors close. The engine starts. The car eases onto the cross street and is gone. Once again, the alley is dark.

But not for long. The window that seemed lighted to me before is lighted again. And Trip was right about business picking up. A few moments later, a young man turns into the alley. By the look of his rain-splattered windbreaker, he's been out in the weather. He reaches into a cellophane packet, draws out the contents, and shoves them in his mouth. He crumples the packet and tosses it aside.

I get my brushes whirring.

"No, Eliot," Trip says. "You don't want him to know you're here."

OK, fine. I'll wait until he leaves.

"Besides, with any luck he didn't eat them all." Trip limps to the packet and noses around in it. He steps back and lifts his head. Orange-colored orts coat his whiskers. He passes a paw over them and licks them off. "Mmm, Cheezy-Ohs. I don't care for the oversized crispy parts. Tough on the choppers. But I like the oily part and the cheese."

His movement gets the boy's attention. He glances down and spits. "Mangy cat. Get outa here." He sticks his foot out and kicks Trip who tumbles into the shadows.

"Trip, are you OK?" I hope so because there's nothing I can do about it if he's not.

17

Trip gets to his three feet and licks the side where the kid kicked him. "Yeah, I'm OK. Ouch. Well, I will be."

"You're right. That was mean," I say. "Is this what you've been living on? Chips?"

"Kinda, yeah. Cookies, too. Beef jerky if I'm lucky. It's not Choice Bites but it's food. Sort of. And there's rats when I can snag 'em. I used to be quite the rat catcher when I was little. It's almost more exercise now than it's worth. Either the little rascals have gotten faster or I've gotten slower. Old age creeping up on me, I guess."

Being short one leg doesn't make it easy and as much as I'd like to reassure Trip, I don't want to embarrass him by mentioning it.

The kid approaches the building with the lighted upper-story window. He pounds on the door, not once but several times. It sounds rhythmic to me and just as I'm wondering if it's some sort of code, the door opens. The young man steps inside and the door closes behind him.

Wherever he went, he wasn't there long. A few minutes later the door reopens and the kid steps outside. The door clangs shut behind him.

Not wasting a moment, the kid slides down the wall and plants his butt on the damp pavement. He opens a little clear plastic bag, sticks his nose in it, and inhales so deeply that not only do the contents get sucked up, the plastic flattens against his nostrils.

Tossing the packet aside, he rests his head against the wall and closes his eyes. Minutes later, he lets out a hysterical laugh. Getting to his feet, he does a clumsy dance, giggling and howling the whole time. He prances around the alley, throwing his head back and punching the air, wiggling his shoulders and hips and kicking his feet, moving to a tune only he can hear. It would be amusing, enchanting, if not for his lips drawn back over his teeth in a sneer, his huge, gleaming eyes, his maniacal cackle.

He passes a tall wheeled waste bin and pauses. Instead of punching the air, he clouts the bin and directs his prancing kicks at it. Made of sturdy steel, the bin withstands the attack. Admitting defeat or maybe simply tiring, the young man hops away favoring one foot, his knuckles dark. He weaves to the mouth of the alley, turns the corner, and disappears.

"Wow, his mood flipped. Like day to night in the blink of any eye," I say to Trip.

"That's the mega," Trip replies. "As high as they get at the start, that's how hostile and violent they become."

Two young women enter the side street. Teenagers, their T-shirts hang on their skinny frames. Thin arms thread through the straps of backpacks dappled with stickers. Knobby knees poke through the holes in their jeans. Long hair streams down one girl's back. Dark and light stripes suggest her hair is streaked, I'm guessing in shades of bright blue, green, and purple as I've seen on TV. The other wears her hair in a sort of Mohawk style, the sides shaven and a crown like a rooster's comb on top. Arms around each other's shoulders, they approach the door and apply the coded knock. As before, a few minutes pass, then the door opens and they go inside.

When they reappear, they stop a few paces from the building.

"Me first," says the girl with the streaked hair.

"Uh uh. You went first the last time," the other replies.

"Yeah, but I saw what happens when you get mega'd. You snorted the whole thing. I may never get a chance."

"Oh, OK," says her Mohawked friend. She hands over the packet.

The streaked girl snorts some of the contents, throws her head back, and hoots. Before she can inhale a second dose her Mohawked pal grabs the package from her. She manages to sniff some of the contents and whoops.

The streaked girl tugs the packet away.

"Gimme that back, bitch," cries Mohawked.

"Who you calling a bitch, you slut?"

"Slut? Why you ..." Mohawked reels back and throws a punch.

I can hear the bone crack when her fist connects with Streaked's yaw.

Streaked falls to the ground but kicks her legs out and topples Mohawked. Streaked throws herself on top of her friend. Entangled, they roll around on the dirty pavement, screaming and scratching.

"I was in a fight like that once," Trip says. "Before I got rescued and brought to the shelter. This big ginger tom wanted me to know whose territory I had invaded. I ended up with a bad abscess. I was lucky; the shelter got a vet who treated the infection."

"I don't understand. Five minutes ago those two girls were best friends."

Trip snickers. "That's what mega does to people. It transforms them."

Chapter Seven

Bleeding, Streaked stumbles out to the cross street.

On her belly, Mohawked slithers on the ground toward the plastic packet. Twisting onto her back, she lifts the packet and pours the remainder into her nose. She stretches out spread-eagled on the pavement for a few minutes, then rolls back onto her stomach and crawls away.

"I don't understand," I tell Trip. "I can understand why they might try it once. But why a second time if they know they'll end up hurting themselves?"

"Because they think it will be different next time. Or they think they can handle it. Or they don't care because the high was worth the pain that follows. Anyway, they don't have much choice. They become hooked after their first use. They've got to have more. Mega creates a very loyal customer base. It's a big money maker for the people who sell it."

For the next hour or so, people straggle into the alley and knock on the door. An unseen host admits them. When they emerge, they don't hesitate but gorge the plastic packets' contents. Their initial frenzied euphoria becomes inexplicable anger resulting in their kicking and punching trash cans and walls. Several limp from the alley, fists crushed and bleeding.

Some are middle-aged or older people whose posture hints they're drunk or high or accustomed to spending a lot of time that way. But most are teens, some pre-teens.

I recall what Officer Flores said about lives ruined. "Trip, that mega is mean stuff."

"Told you. It's not the half of what happens on this street, but it could be the worst."

At last, the lighted window goes dark. Not long after, two men emerge from the building, one carrying a box. He tosses it away. It tumbles and lands on one side, its flaps open. Neither ecstatic nor manic, the two men stroll from the alley.

"The dealers," Trip says. "They're sellers, not users." 'He trots over to sniff the box and bats it with a paw. "Oh, boy, a box." He looks at me and smiles. "I love boxes." He lifts a foreleg to get in.

"Wait, Trip. Who knows what they were using the box for? They could have been carrying the mega in it. You don't know, it could be contaminated."

Too late. Trip springs into the box.

"Trip! Don't inhale anything. You saw what mega did to the people in the alley. The effect on you could be much worse."

"Hmph."

"Trip, don't lick your paw. Get out of that box. Get over here."

With a grunt, Trip leaps out of the box with as much grace as a tripod cat can manage.

"Lie on your back. Stick out your paws and get the pads under my brushes. Let me clean them."

"You don't think—?"

"I don't want to take any chances."

Trip flips over. He doesn't have much of a belly, not like Chloe. Poor guy. A diet of Cheezy-Ohs and cookies isn't doing him much good.

I dust his paws as best I can. "I think you're clean," I tell him.

"Define clean," he says. He settles on his haunches and licks his chest.

"Business," as Trip called it, withers to a trickle. People still come calling for mega. Noticing the window is dark, some turn and slink away. Others knock on the door, at first with measured deliberation. When no one answers, they hammer harder. Still getting no response, they pound on the door with both fists and kick it. Admitting defeat, they spit and swear and stomp off.

At last, we're alone in the alley. Trip meanders to a pile of crushed boxes draped with a rag. "It has been a long night. I'm going to bed," he says. He pads around on the boxes and snuggles into the rag.

"I thought cats prowl at night," I reply.

"Wrong-o. I don't know where we got that reputation. We're not nocturnal, we're crepuscular."

"Huh? Is that, like, old or something?"

"It means we're active at dusk and dawn." Trip yawns, showing jaws lined with sharp teeth. "I can't remember when my last nap was. You going to be OK?"

"Oh, sure. I'll shift into snooze mode. I've had a long day too." It wouldn't hurt to conserve my power. I hope my batteries won't run down while I rest.

A noise startles me out of sleeping mode. Not only am I not in my docking station, I'm not in the Lady's cottage. I'm in some downtrodden alleyway. Dawn's early light shows me this street has been sorely neglected.

That noise ... *is it Alexa telling me to start cleaning?*

No, it's a cat prowling around. Trip wasn't kidding about being active at dawn. The sun hasn't fully risen and he's poking his nose into corners.

"Trip?"

"Oh, hey, did I wake you?"

"No," I lie. "Whatcha doin'?"

"Reconnoitering. Making sure nothing's different and everything is where it was yesterday. If something is in a different place, I need to know about it."

I shouldn't be surprised. When the Lady gets a new piece of furniture or a rug or a plant, Chloe is cranky for days. She expresses her discontent by clawing the new item or peeing on it. That does not please the Lady who didn't understand she had altered Chloe's environment.

It could explain why Trip hasn't ventured from this street although it's rough and hostile. Relocating would mean change and he doesn't like change.

I'm not delighted about new items either. I'm programmed to follow a particular route. I at least have collision sensors that help me avoid new obstacles.

"I'm also looking for something to eat. Seeing if any of the nighttime visitors left me goodies."

"People came by at night?"

"Oh, yeah. You saw. It's not like the mega drugstore keeps regular hours. People come by all hours, day and night, hoping they'll find the sellers. Plus, the mega drugstore isn't the only thing happening here. This is a busy place."

Chapter Eight

As Trip speaks, a figure enters the street from the outlet at the end. Shrouded in a hooded field jacket, he scours the gutter. Coming up with a plastic packet, he tries to inhale the contents. He glares at it and grumbling, crumbles it and tosses it aside.

Spotting an abandoned wire shopping cart, he creeps toward it and tugs it toward him. I can hear the wheels squeak.

A lump in a doorway moves. Wrapped in a torn and stained raincoat, a skinny grizzled man struggles to his feet. "Hey! That's mine!"

Half leaning on, half pushing the cart, the field jacket guy breaks into a trot.

"Get back here!" The raincoat man charges after him as fast as the flopping soles of his splitting shoes will allow.

"Now what's that all about?" I ask Trip. "The man in the raincoat—did he sleep here all night?"

"Wouldn't surprise me. He could have taken too much mega and passed out. More likely though, he's a homeless guy. He had nowhere to go."

"Why spend the night here out in the weather? On the concrete? Couldn't he find a bench somewhere?"

"Homeless people are considered vagrants. Police shoo them out of city parks, off bus benches, and out of store doorways."

"Why not arrest them, put them in jail for the night? At least they'd be indoors, have a cot to sleep on, food to eat."

"It's not a crime to be homeless. Well, I guess, in a way, it is a crime. What I mean is, it's not illegal."

"It's too bad there aren't shelters for them, like for animals."

"Oh, there are. A lot of homeless people don't like them. They say they're crowded, which they likely are. Homelessness is a big problem that no one wants to talk about or do anything about. It's the same for stray cats and dogs. People's shelters are as crammed as animal shelters.

"I told you, I spent some time in the animal shelter. I'm not griping. The managers kept dogs and cats separate. And there were a lot of volunteers. They made sure we had fresh water and food. Cleaned our litter boxes. Cuddled us and brushed us. There was even a volunteer vet who took care of any sick or injured animals.

"Sure, sardined together like that stressed some of the rescues and made them short-tempered. Fights broke out. The volunteers stopped them before anyone got seriously hurt. I don't have anything bad to say about the animal shelter. It wasn't ideal but it sure beat living on the street."

"Like you're doing now."

Trip sighs. "Good point."

"Why not get yourself to a shelter again? It sounds like it was pleasant. You have good memories of your experience."

"Ah, but it was in another city. It's a different story here. The shelter I was in was a no-kill shelter. This one, you get five days. If you're not claimed by then ..." He draws a paw across his neck, makes a husky croaking sound in his throat, and collapses on his back.

"Trip, that's mean!"

He rises to sit on his haunches. "That's how it is in this city. They say it's because of overcrowding, they can't afford to keep an animal for longer than that. You can understand why I stay hidden. I don't want to get nabbed by Animal Control.

"Shelters for people have their share of problems too. They have curfews and don't allow alcohol. Some of the homeless people don't like the rules. They'd rather be on their own so they can come and go as they please. They complain the few possessions they do have get stolen."

"That man, he didn't have any better luck here."

Trip snorts. "I told you this was a mean street."

"You weren't in the shelter long, were you?"

"A few months. The people who run the shelter put a lot of effort into finding fur-ever homes for the animals. We had an open house when the public was invited to tour the facility. Fundraising was the main goal but it was also a way to show us off. The volunteers made sure we were all cleaned and groomed and on our best behavior. Some of us got to wear ribbons around our necks. I didn't hold out much hope. I had to compete with cute kittens and I was almost two. But to my surprise, I got adopted out the next day."

"You must have been happy to leave the shelter."

Trip gives his leg a lick. "I was and I wasn't. It was strange at first. I kind of missed all the activity and the playmates and the shelter volunteers. They were so sweet to me. But after I got adopted, I didn't have to shove any noses out of my food bowl. The lady, she spoiled me. She brushed me every day and entertained me with feather-teaser toys. She fed me yummy tuna paté from tiny cans and gave me treats.

"I liked her little boy, too. She taught him that pets, even small ones, aren't toys. He helped her clean the litter box. He griped about how smelly it was. Well, it is; that's why it needs frequent cleaning. She told him how important it was to keep it fresh. He got the message because he went back and redid it himself so it got an extra clean."

Extra clean. I can't find any fault with that.

Trip squeezes his eyes and sighs. "The thing was, I couldn't go outside. The lady, she was too worried that I'd get hurt. I could sit on the window sill and watch the world go by but I couldn't get out in it. Cats ..." He grunts. "We always want to be on the other side of the door. We don't care what's there, we want to be on the other side of it."

"Curiosity killed the cat. Isn't that how the saying goes?"

Trip gives me a thoughtful look. "Yeah, well, there may be something to that. Anyhow, it turns out she was right. I did get out one night and got hit by a car and, well, here I am."

"You know a lot about what happens on this street. About people."

"I learn a lot by listening. People talk. They don't notice that I'm listening. You know, people don't think cats understand speech. We do. We only pretend we don't. That way we can disregard any commands or instructions we don't like. Like, 'get off the counter' or 'don't scratch the sofa' or —this is my favorite—'oh, no, don't barf on the carpet.'"

Now why didn't I think of that? I could ignore Alexa when she calls me "Stupid." If I function only when she addresses me with respect, she'll change her ways. When I get home, I'll have to find a way to inform her that my name is "Eliot," not "Stupid."

Chapter Nine

A man staggers into the street from the outlet. He wears a coat that is open despite the cold breeze. He holds one arm straight out as if to keep his balance. The other hangs at his side. Clutched in his hand is a brown paper sack.

He leans against the brick wall and slides down to a sitting position. He unwraps the paper's twisted top and holds the sack to his mouth. The Adam's apple in his neck moves up and down. He's swallowing the contents.

Setting down the sack, he upchucks, then folds in on himself. His eyes close and he slumps to lie on his side.

"Trip! Did that man die right before our eyes?" That would be mean.

"Not likely. I doubt he's dead; he passed out. He's a drunk. He polished off a whole bottle of some rot-gut booze. He'll sleep it off. Then he'll go buy more. He'll be back. He'll get some mega, too. And he's not the only one."

I consider the pool of puke. I've never cleaned up vomit before. I suppose I could mop it. I move in that direction.

"Where are you going?" Trip asks.

"To clean that. Shouldn't I clean it?"

"Nah. It'll dry up. Rats and ants will take care of most of it. It'll get washed away the next time it rains." Trip springs to his feet, his ears laid back. "Quick, go hide under that trash can."

Three kids turn into the street. Not much older than the teen girls who bought mega yesterday, they too have backpacks. The boys' outfits are almost identical. The hems of their baggy pants drag so low I can't figure out how they walk without tripping. Oversized loose T-shirts

29

drape to their knees. Red bandanas wrapped around their heads are topped by ball caps worn to the side or backward.

Their shirts bear symbols I recognize from TV.

"Look at how they're dressed. They're sports fans. They follow the same team. Are they members of a fan club?" I ask Trip.

"Not a club. A gang. They may be fans of that team but that's not why they wear those clothes. It's a cheap, convenient way to show off a gang trademark. It's not like they can order designer clothes with their custom logo. There are two gangs in this area and they compete with each other for turf. Kind of the way that ginger tom thought he controlled his territory. You and I better hide. They wouldn't hesitate to kick or step on you or me for fun."

Like the homeless men, the kids search the street for mega packets. Unlike the homeless men, they have better luck. They score enough packets to get a few sniffs.

Perhaps galvanized by the drug and with athleticism that under other circumstances would be admirable, one youth scales the wall of the ground floor building to access its flat roof. From his backpack, he pulls out a spray paint can and applies designs on the wall of the second story. Huge swirls obliterate the existing markings.

"See what I mean?" Trip says. "That'll last about a day. Then the other gang will see it and have to come in and put their tag over it." He chuckles. "I don't know which is worse: the ginger cat spraying to mark his territory or gang graffiti. The paint smells as strong as the cat pee."

I have no sense of smell but I do know the Lady goes berserk when Chloe marks something. Griping out loud, the Lady squirts detergents, blots the stain, and discards the rags she uses. She scolds Chloe who either doesn't hear or doesn't care.

The boy descends to the street and the trio steps back to admire the work.

Now that was mean, covering up someone else's work. *And how will I clean that off?* I can't even get up there. I could mop it except I'd have to position myself vertically and somehow scale the wall.

I'm mulling over how I'll tackle this new challenge when Trip groans. "Uh oh, here comes trouble."

From the mouth of the street, another trio arrives. Like the other boys, they wear caps, bandanas, long T-shirts, and baggy pants. These boys' bandanas are blue, not red. The hems of their wide pants are cut off to display their high-top sneakers. "Are they members of the same gang?" I ask Trip.

"Oh, heck, no. Check them out. Their bandanas are blue, not red. And their logos are for a different team. In other words, a different gang. We're gonna have a fight on our hands, for sure."

The second trio stops. One of their members takes a step forward. The other two stand shoulder to shoulder at his back, forming a triangle. The blue team leader yells "Yo. What you think you're doing?"

The three red team members whip around and for a second freeze in place. Then they too form a triangle. "This be our turf," their leader hollers. "You got no business here."

I learn why their clothes are so roomy. From the copious depths, they draw an arsenal of weapons: knives, lengths of chain, brass knuckles, and blackjacks.

"Oh yeah?" comes the reply. "We show you."

Without another word, the blue team leader rushes forward, his teammates one step behind.

The red team advances.

"Why don't they run away instead of running into it?" I ask Trip. "If they go now, they can escape."

"That's not going to happen," Trip drawls.

The human arrowheads aim for each other and collide in the middle of the street.

Arms, legs, and chains flail. Caps fly off. Blades flash in the morning light. Screams of surprise, anger, and pain bounce off the walls. Fabric tears, bones crack. The reds and blues become so entangled the melee looks purple.

A red team member sinks to the ground, clutching his leg. He cries out when one of the combatants tramples him and he wriggles a few inches from the knot. Then, yelling with fury, he rolls into the tangle, tripping one of the blue team members who falls onto his back. A red team member throws himself on top of the prone blue. Arms swinging, he throws punches.

The other four pile on. It's a huddle like what I've seen during football matches the Lady watches on TV only there's nothing sporting about this. No medics stand by to mend broken noses or limbs.

One by one the combatants roll off, clutching an arm, a leg, a head until two are left. A red team member rises to his knees, scrambles to his feet, and charges for the exit. One of his team members hobbles behind him. The third lies in the street, not moving.

Chapter Ten

Blood running down his face, the blue team leader tugs at his torn and stained shirt. "We showed 'em, boys. They won't be back. They know whose turf this be."

His gang members gather the scattered paint cans. Hoisted up by his pals, the leader mounts the roof and covers the recently applied graffiti with fresh markings. Launching himself to the ground, he approaches the prostrate red gang member. Standing over the body, he aims the spray can at the figure and covers it with blue paint. He tosses the can onto the body and wipes his hands on his shirt. "Let's go, boys."

He and his cohorts turn to the exit. Creeping and limping, they leave trails of blood. I realize the dark splotches I noticed earlier weren't oil or antifreeze drippings from previous traffic but rather dried bloodstains from gang warfare.

"Aren't they going to help him?" I ask Trip.

I get no reply and spin to find Trip curled in a ball, snoring.

"Trip?" I give him a gentle nudge.

Trip comes immediately awake. It must be a cat thing; I've seen Chloe spring from sound asleep onto all four paws in an instant.

"What?" he asks.

"That boy. He's hurt. And his friends left him there."

"Don't feel too sorry for him. He's young. He'll heal. Besides, he'll be proud of his injuries. Battle scars. They'll add to his street cred, show he was in a fight and lived to tell about it."

The lone red gang member stirs. Looking around him, he sees he is alone in the alley. He rises to an elbow and drags himself down the street, leaving a streak in his wake, part paint, part spilled blood.

I scurry over, get my brushes and mop spinning.

"What are you doing?" Trip asks.

"I'm going to clean it."

"Don't bother. You'll never get all that up. Besides, what are you going to do about the stains? They're set."

He's right. *How am I going to clean this mean street?* It would take stronger chemicals than what I have on board to remove the vestiges of past battles.

I don't have what it takes. The boss picked the wrong man for the job. *What was he thinking? What was I thinking?* I should go back to the Lady's cottage and stick to wiping household floors.

"Besides," Trip says, "They'll be back. Those red guys won't take this insult lying down, no pun intended. They've still got to show this is their turf."

"Why? Why go to so much trouble, endure so much pain, for this street? There are tons of streets in the city. Why don't they move to a different one? Aren't there enough streets to go around?"

"They have a rep to uphold. Besides, this is the street with the mega dealers. The blue kids and the red kids, they're all hooked on mega."

The morning wears on. What I can see of the sky lightens. A car pulls partway into the alley and stops. Through the glass, I see two occupants, a male and a female. They draw closer. The female dips her head below the dashboard. A few minutes pass and her head rises up into my line of view. After another interval, the passenger door opens and she gets out.

The engine restarts, the car backs out of the alley onto the cross street and drives away.

Dressed in a fur-trimmed puffy jacket that doesn't quite extend to the hem of her short skirt, and shoes with heels so high I wonder how she can walk, she counts the bills gripped in her hand. Demonstrating she can indeed walk in those shoes, she picks her way to the steel door. She raps her knuckles in the distinctive rhythm. She waits a few minutes. When no one opens the door, she lifts her shoulders in a shrug. Tucking the money into her jacket's inner pocket, she leaves the alley and turns the corner.

"She's not done," Trip says. "We'll see her again a few times today and later tonight. She's a hard-working girl."

"What is she working at?" I wonder if this is what the Lady does when she leaves the cottage to go to work.

"Servicing her customers. The red gang and the blue gang may have an ongoing feud over whose turf this is but it's also her turf. She stands out on the corner. Curb-crawlers pick her up and come here for a quickie."

"A quick what?"

"Sex. I don't know how much they pay her for her services but it adds up. I'd say she turns ten tricks a day, maybe more. Men on the way to and from work, on their lunch hour. Happy hour before they go home to the wife and kids. And all through the night, of course. She also sells them mega. That saves her customers the trouble of having to come by here hoping the dealers will be doing business."

Trip tsks. "She wouldn't have to work so hard if she didn't have a mega habit herself but I've seen her sniff the stuff. She may have once had a regular life. a job, or even a husband. Who knows? Until she got hooked on mega and had to find a way to supplement her income and support her habit."

"Sex for money? Isn't that illegal?" It is on the TV shows the Lady watches.

"It is."

"Why don't the cops do something about it?"

"They'd have to catch her in the act. And if they did it would create a problem for her customers, some of whom are important people. I suspect the cops know what she's up to. She pays them to look the other way, with favors or packets of mega."

"She bribes the cops?"

"I know she does. I've seen them come by in their patrol cars. They'll roll down the window and she'll hand them the drugs, or, if it's sex they want, she'll get in the car with them. How they do it with all that equipment they've got in there I do not know. Nor do I want to know."

"The cops are bent?" The boss said as much. No wonder he thought I was the man for the job. I have no interest in either sex or drugs. I feel less incompetent. All I need to do now is figure out how to clean this mean street. And I'll have to do it myself. Except for Officers Jameson and Flores, I won't be able to count on the police for assistance. They're all corrupt!

Chapter Eleven

From the outlet, two kids turn into the alley. Like the gang members and the teenage girls, they have backpacks slung over their shoulders. Also like the gang members they wear identical clothing although these two are more formal, outfitted in white shirts, dark slacks, and neckties. They're younger, too.

"Are they members of yet another gang?" I ask Trip.

"Kind of. They go to a private school. I figure it must be nearby because they use this street as a shortcut. They're wearing the school uniform. All the kids who attend the school dress that way. Well, the girls wear skirts instead of pants."

"What are they doing here in the middle of the day?"

"They're on their lunch break."

"Doesn't their school have a place where they can eat?"

"I don't doubt it. But they want more privacy. You'll see."

The shorter of the youngsters has round red cheeks. His unruly hair sticks straight up from the top of his head. His companion is taller and thinner and appears a year or two older. Two silvery dots bracket one of his eyebrows. They resemble what the Lady wears although I don't know why they are on the kid's face and not his earlobe.

"Go knock on that door," the taller one says to the shorter one. "Do it just the way I told you."

The little guy trots to the steel door, delivers the idiosyncratic knock, and stands and waits. When it goes unanswered he tries again. After the third try, he shrugs his shoulders and joins his pal.

"No one's home, I guess," the little boy says.

"You knocked exactly like I told you?" asks his pal.

"I did. Honest."

The taller boy twitches his eyebrows. "They're not here. We'll have to chill until they show up."

They find a somewhat clean spot where they can sit with their backs against the brick wall. They slip off their backpacks and empty them onto the ground. Like the drunk, they have brown paper sacks. Unlike the drunk, these sacks are smaller. I'm guessing they're sandwich bags. I've seen the Lady prepare these to take to work sometimes.

The kids don't open the bags. Instead, the younger one removes a bottle from one of the backpacks. Filled with clear liquid, it resembles the empty ones rolling around. He hands it to his buddy who unscrews the top and takes a long drink. "Where'd you get this?" he asks.

"Like you said to do. Look in the parents' liquor cabinet. You sure my dad's not going to miss it?"

"I bet not. You way you talk about him, he won't even notice. Or he'll figure he drank it himself." He passes the bottle to the other kid who swallows some.

The younger boy makes a face. "I don't know what you all see in this. It tastes terrible."

"It grows on you," his friend replies. "Plus, you get to like how you feel when you've had some. It's not as good as mega but it'll do until we can score." He picks up a palm-sized package. He tips it out but it doesn't yield a cigarette like I've seen on TV. I'm glad. Those two seem young to be smoking.

Instead of a tightly rolled white cylinder, the pack yields something that looks handmade. The older kid flicks another tube, a pink one about the size of a finger. It emits a small flame which he applies to the white cylinder. Putting it in his mouth he takes a deep breath. Holding his breath, he passes the cylinder to his younger pal who does the same.

"See?" Trip says. "They can't do that in the school cafeteria."

"Do what?"

"Drink booze and smoke dope," Trip replies.

"But ... but they're kids."

"Getting an early start down the road to ruin," Trip says. "You heard him. Stole it from his father. Alcohol and pot are the least of their problems. They're into mega, too."

"Don't we need to get back?" asks the younger boy. "Won't they wonder where we went?"

His friend shakes his head. "They didn't even notice. I'll bet there aren't any monitors in the lunchroom today. All the teachers got called to a special assembly for active shooter response training."

"Why doesn't someone do anything to stop them?" I ask Trip.

"Like who?" Trip replies. "The parents and the teachers have got their own problems."

Well, someone should. *It's up to me, I guess, but how?* I take an inventory of the tools I have at my disposal but none are of any use for this problem.

The school kids take turns drinking and smoking until the bottle is empty and the weed is a stub the size of a fingernail clipping. Struggling to their feet, they sling on the backpacks and stagger from the alley.

"But ... but, they left their lunch bags." I start after them.

"Where are you going?" Trip asks.

"Maybe I can get their attention and they'll realize they forgot them."

Trip says, "They don't care." He trots over to the abandoned bag and with his nose, nudges it open. He sticks a paw in the bag and drags out a small package wrapped in white paper. Snagging the paper with a claw he pulls the wrapping apart and sniffs. "Oh, goody!" he cries. "Tuna salad. I love tuna!" He swacks away the top bread layer and licks the filling.

While Trip sleeps off his lunch, I cruise the street. I wish there were a way to clean it, to make it nicer and homier for Trip since he plans to live out the rest of his life here. Plastic packets are flattened against the curb and the buildings' footings. I won't attempt to vacuum those up. The plastic would clog my suction port and I have no idea what the contents would do to my mechanism.

I can't clear away the blotches staining the pavement. I can't ascend the walls and wipe off the graffiti. *What good am I?*

Chapter Twelve

I mosey to the end, to the outlet opposite the mouth of the alley where I first entered. Peering down one side I discover why the building on the alley's right is nothing but a windowless brick wall. The side facing the cross street is the same: no windows, only a series of wide tall roll-up doors. It doesn't need windows; it's a self-storage unit. The Lady brought me to one like it. She wanted me to clean the floor before she brought over her belongings.

This one takes up an entire block. A wide asphalt driveway separates it from the road. As I watch, pickup trucks and cars pull out of traffic and back up to the doors.

I swivel to face the other direction. On the cross street side of the one-story building with the clerestory windows, a panel hanging from a wooden frame swings in the breeze. The panel bears lettering and the photo of a smiling man holding out a key. I can't read but I've watched enough TV to know this is a sign for a Realtor. Whoever owns or is in charge of the building wants passersby to know it's vacant and available to be leased or bought.

Farther along, signs hang from awnings or atop poles stretching to the sky. I don't know what the signs say but I understand what some of them mean. In front of one shop, red and blue stripes twine diagonally up a rotating white pillar, signifying a barber works there. Three gold balls hang from a beam extending from the establishment next to it. I believe that indicates a pawnbroker. A carved statue stands next to the door of another storefront. It is the figure of a man shielding his eyes with his hands and wearing feathers on top of his head. I'm not sure about that one; maybe that's a sculptor's studio. I'm more confident about the one displaying a big white cup with a handle. That's either a coffeehouse or a café.

A multistory building fills the block opposite the shops. Old by virtue of its gray chipped façade it has many windows but only one entrance. Barbeque grills and bicycles crowd the balconies below the windows and laundry drapes the rusted metal frames.

Cars and trucks ply the road at a steady pace. Kids wearing backpacks and women toting large purses leave the apartment building; others return carting sacks with bread loaves poking out the top or shirts on hangers. Shoppers enter the storefronts or emerge carrying boxes and bags.

Looking neither right nor left, they're all going about their day as if nothing is wrong. *Are they oblivious to the abysmal meanness pervading the alley only a few feet away? Do they know about the mega dealers, the gang members, the homeless and the hookers, the truants, the corrupt cops?*

Are they automatons? Robots who can do only what they are programmed to do, like me in a former life?

"The city's counting on you, Eliot," the boss said. It's my job to clean up the mean street and I can see why. These people either don't know or don't care or don't know what to do about it or have given up.

But how? I circle and gaze in despair down the length of the alley, at the soiled pavement, the defaced walls.

Trip's awake and scouring the kids' lunch bags.

"Have you ever made it past that door?" I ask him.

"Hmm, chips," he says, and claws the bag. "I have. I didn't go far. At the rear of a short vestibule, another door opens to a hallway. A flight of metal stairs takes up the rest of the space. Those lead to a landing and more stairs to yet another floor. I didn't prowl around. I didn't want to get too far from the entry door and get trapped in the building. Seems to me, though, whatever's going on in there happens on some upper floor. I could make it up those stairs. I haven't had a good reason."

"But the mean stuff. That's where it starts, upstairs. That's like the base camp."

Trip swishes his tail. "None of my business."

But it is mine. I'm supposed to clean up these mean streets. The boss ordered me. The city counts on me. If upstairs is the epicenter that's where I need to be. *How, though?*

Trip can mount stairs, he just doesn't want to. I don't blame him. Missing a leg makes it hard work. I can't at all. I can fall down them, I've learned that much. But I can't ascend them.

Throughout the day, mega customers young and old come calling. When their hammering goes unanswered, they kick or pound the door. Muttering and cursing, they slouch away. Some return an hour or so later, to no avail.

As Trip predicted, the working girl makes several visits.

A police car cruises a few feet down the alley and pauses but no one gets out. After idling a few minutes, it reverses out.

I keep watch while Trip sleeps through it all.

Daylight dwindles and true to his crepuscular self, Trip wakes up. In the fading light, he makes the rounds, noting any changes and scrounging for something to eat.

Nightfall doesn't reduce the activity. If anything, it picks up. The street gets meaner by the minute but I still haven't figured out how I can clean it.

Chapter Thirteen

Two men, one big and tall, the other small and slender, stride into the alley and approach the door.

Dressed in a hoodie and floppy gym shorts and carrying a large box, the smaller one sniffles.

"Hey, what's this doing here, Mota?" he asks.

"What?" replies the other man. Taller, also wearing a hoodie, Mota has got some years on the other guy. Long scraggly hair covers the top of his head and an equally scraggly beard blankets his chin. Tattoos sprawl across his forehead as well as his fingers between the middle and base knuckles. They're letters but I don't know what they spell.

The younger man sets his box down, leans over, stretches out an arm, and picks me up. "This." He holds me out for the other man to see.

"I dunno. Like, a frisbee?"

"No. Ya know what this is? This is one of them robot cleaners. You program it and it goes around vacuuming even if you're not there."

"What you want that for? Like you do a lot of vacuuming," Mota scoffs.

The younger man sniffles again. Maybe he has a cold. "And you do? What I'm sayin' is, these things ain't cheap. I can maybe pawn it, sell it, get something for it."

"Ok. Whatever. Come on, Sneeze. We got work to do." Mota approaches the door. I expect him to rap out the coded message the way everyone else has.

Good luck, Chump. Like everyone else today, you're about to be disappointed.

Instead, he puts a key in the lock and the door opens.

He has a key? He could be the Realtor, the building's owner or a tenant, a security guard, or a janitor. His disreputable appearance has me thinking he's the mega dealer.

He holds the door ajar. "You coming?"

"Yeah." Sneeze replaces me on the ground, collects his box, and steps toward the door.

With a name like Sneeze, this young guy must have a respiratory problem. Perhaps he has a dust allergy. He ought to keep me. I could help him control the particulates in his environment.

Sneeze turns, picks me up, and lays me on top of the box. He follows Mota toward the open door.

"Trip! Trip! Help! I'm being kidnapped," I wail.

"Don't worry, Eliot. I'll come find you."

Trip was right, there is a flight of stairs. The men start up, reach a landing, and mount another flight leading to a hallway.

Part of me panics. *How will I ever get out?* I can override my cliff sensors and tumble down all those stairs but I'm not likely to survive the fall. Even if I do there's the problem of getting that heavy steel door open and keeping it open while I squeeze through.

But, part of me is elated. I'm being escorted into the Hub of Meanness. This is my chance, my shot at fulfilling the mission the boss gave me.

In the hallway, Sneeze and Mota pull brown paper sandwich bags from their pockets. They open them and set them on the floor, but instead of removing sandwiches, they step into the bags and twist the tops around their ankles. They wriggle their hands into filmy gloves.

Hmm. On TV, police officers cover their hands and shoes to prevent leaving finger- and footprints. *Could these two men be policemen? In those outfits?* They could be undercover. That could explain why they brought me along. They must know the boss assigned me to clean up. They're my partners. Hey, fellas!

Mota opens a door and the two men enter. Sneeze puts his box on the floor and holds up his phone. Light fills a room. A folding table with a white plastic top leans against a wall. Other than that, the space is devoid of furnishings.

This can't be the Hub of Meanness. The only mean thing about it is its decrepitude. Bare and battered, the dirty tile floor is scuffed and so thin in spots, the mastic shows through. The gypsum walls are faded and dusty. Darker colored rectangles indicate where pictures once hung; all that remains are the holes left by the hooks. Dents mark where a chair back or maybe a fist collided with the wall. In spots, entire chunks of wallboard are missing, exposing the timber framing and insulation.

This is far from the shiny chrome and glossy lacquer of the Lady's cottage. *Did people live in this filth and decay?* That's mean. I can't do anything about the necessary repairs but I could clean it. *Is that what I'm meant to do? Has it all been leading to this?*

Mota drags the table to the center of the room, unfolds the legs, and stands it up. Sneeze sets the box on top. He also produces a lamp. It's either battery-operated or USB-charged because he turns it on without plugging it in anywhere. Clever thinking since this apartment doesn't appear to have electric service. It's a good thing the lightning strike supercharged me. Even if I had my docking station, plugging it in here wouldn't do any good.

Mota opens the box's flaps. He unzips his hoodie to reveal a firearm tucked into the waistband of his jeans. "OK, we're ready for business, Sneeze. Go get the first customer."

My question has been answered. These are not undercover police officers, they are the mega dealers.

With a sniffle, Sneeze leaves the room closing the door behind him. After a few minutes, I hear the same signature rap I heard downstairs. One hand poised on his gun, Mota takes a packet from the box. The packet resembles the one I saw the young man sniff from that first rainy night in the alley and the one the two girls fought over. I assume this is mega. Mota opens the door. Exchanging the packet for a fistful of bills, he closes the door.

This goes on for a while. The selling and buying continue for the length of time it takes me to do a room: about fifteen minutes.

The rap at the door sounds insistent. Mota opens it to Sneeze.

"Cops on their way," Sneeze says, storming into the room. "We gotta get outa here."

Sneeze stows the lamp. Mota collapses the table and stands it against the wall. They grab their box and race toward the door. Almost as an afterthought, Sneeze returns to the room and seizes me. While I'm not delighted to be adopted by a drug dealer, I'm grateful I wasn't abandoned in that room. *Who knows how long I'd be there?*

They strip off the hand and foot covers. Their footsteps resound as they charge down the stairs to the ground floor.

Mota twists the deadbolt lock and flings the door open. Sneeze and Mota dart out the door and stop so abruptly they slam into each other.

Chapter Fourteen

Standing side-by-side, two figures face the door, their legs spread shoulder-width apart.

"Stop! Stop right there! Police officers!" they chorus and hold out badges.

"Put down the box," says the tall one.

It's Officer Flores!

"Hands above your heads," says his partner whom I recognize as Officer Jameson.

Snapping to attention, Sneeze drops the box and me. I land on my wheels, shaken but not shattered.

A shape moves toward me. My motor cycles. In a crouch, Trip crawls to my side. "Are you OK?"

"Yeah. That was a jolt all right but I'm not cracked or anything."

Sneeze shoots his hands up high and stands rigid and sniffling. His posture more relaxed, Mota raises his arms so his hands are about level with his ears.

"Don't take your eyes off them, Jameson," says Officer Flores. "Let me see what's in this box." He bends over, peers into the carton, and chortles. "Well, I'll be. It's full of mega packets." He straightens. "Jameson, we got 'em." His voice throbs with triumph.

With his foot, Officer Flores shoves the box behind Officer Jameson. Standing at her side he faces the drug dealers. "I'm Officer Flores and you two are under arrest. Possession with intent to sell. Officer Jameson, 'cuff 'em and escort the suspects to the car. Get their names, ID. Call it in. And pop the trunk."

Officer Jameson moves behind Sneeze. "Lower your arms, please," she says, more polite than I would have been had I been in her shoes. "Put your hands behind your back."

With a sniffle, Sneeze complies. I hear a metallic click. Her hand between his shoulder blades, Officer Jameson steers Sneeze toward the police car. She guides him into the back seat and closes the door. Opening the trunk, she sets the box inside. She slams the trunk lid closed and leans against the cruiser, a satisfied grin on her face.

Officer Flores removes handcuffs from his utility belt. To Mota, he says, "You too. Hands behind your back."

"Like hell I will," Mota says. "Imma kill you, copper." He whips out his gun.

Officer Jameson darts from the cruiser to aid Officer Flores. "Put down the gun," she hollers.

Seizing his opportunity, Sneeze springs from the cruiser and chugs down the alley.

Mota raises his gun and points it at Officer Flores.

No! Oh, no! My comrade is in mortal danger.

I rev my motor and charge. Overriding my obstacle avoidance, I slam against Mota's ankle.

"Ouch. What the—?" he roars and he fires but I've unbalanced him. He stumbles and lands on his butt. The gun flies from his hand.

The bullet misses Officer Flores and dings a trash can. The ring is followed by an agonized cry of pain that ricochets off the buildings' walls and echoes down the alley. Someone was hit!

It wasn't Officer Jameson. She scoops up the gun and charges down the alley after the escaping Sneeze.

Officer Flores has Mota pressed against the building. Wrestling with him, Officer Flores manacles Mota and manhandles him toward the cruiser. Officer Flores isn't injured nor is Mota.

"You are in big trouble now, Buster," Officer Flores says to Mota. "Threatening a police officer with gun. That's aggravated assault with a deadly weapon. You are going down!"

Sneeze in tow, Officer Jameson returns to the cruiser. No longer polite, she shoves him into the back seat and slams the door shut. "Now stay there!" she hollers.

Neither of the officers nor suspects appear injured. But, that howl ... no one else is in the alley except ...

Oh, no! The bullet ricocheted off the trash can and hit Trip. *Where is he?*

Officer Flores loads Mota into the rear of the cruiser and gets behind the wheel. The engine starts. The headlights glow. Officer Flores backs the cruiser down the alley. Light washes the pavement ahead, the side of the building. The alley dims as Flores turns the cruiser and advances down the street. Then even the red rear lights vanish leaving the alley in the shadows but not before I spot a shape even darker than the night sky. Pressed against the wall's base, it moves.

"Trip?"

I edge closer. It is Trip, lying on his side. I slow. I want to race to him to see if he needs help but part of me doesn't want to know.

I hear a low moan and speed forward. "Trip, are you OK?" I angle so my headlight skims his body. Burned fur carves a streak across his side. "You were hit."

He rises to a crouch. "Yeah. I'm OK. It's just a flesh wound."

The trail gleams in my headlight. The bullet may have only grazed him but it scorched his fur and broke his skin and he's bleeding. "I don't like the looks of it, Trip."

He wets a paw and gives it a listless swipe. "I can't ... reach it."

"We've got to find help, Trip. Where can we go? Who can help? I don't know this area at all."

What are we going to do? I've been in trouble before, hung up on a doorsill, tangled in a throw rug, or hamstrung by a loose thread wrapped around my nose wheel. Admitting defeat, I grind to a halt and sound a plaintive beep. The Lady comes and untangles me and gets me restarted.

Even if I could find someone and beep at them, they would have no idea what the trouble is. *How can I draw someone's attention, much less get them to the alley to treat Trip?*

I scan the street. Mega customers won't know their suppliers have been arrested. They'll continue to come and knock on the door. When they get no answer, they'll turn and leave. They won't notice an injured cat and even if they do, they won't care.

Chapter Fifteen

"Trip, Trip. I've got an idea." I've seen this done on the TV. The Lady sometimes views a channel of miscellaneous assorted videos. Chloe's never tried what I've seen demonstrated but the cats on the videos seem to enjoy it. "Let's go get help."

"Us? You? How?"

"Climb up on my back. Tell me where to go and I'll carry you."

Trip pads over and arranges himself on my lid.

I start my motor and aim for the mouth of the alley. Trip isn't huge but I'm unused to having any burden at all and I find his weight a load. It takes all the energy I can muster to move.

"I've checked some of this out before. A lot of small shops line the street to the left. Maybe we'll find a big-hearted human."

"I dunno, Eliot. What if the shop owner thinks I'm a stray and calls Animal Control?"

"I didn't think of that." I study the signs. *Which of those stores would likely house a human who would be sympathetic about an injured cat?* "To our right is a self-storage building."

"Self-storage? Like a warehouse? Maybe we should try to get in. Warehouses tend to have rodent problems. I'll bet that's where all the rats and mice I've been eating have been coming from."

"We should stay clear of it, Trip. If there are rats there might also be other cats. What if there are and they want to pick a fight with you? You're in no shape to fight back. Plus, the vehicles coming in and out move faster than we can. We're likely to get run over. I think our best option is the left."

With a sigh, Trip stretches out on my lid, his chin propped above my headlight, his legs draped over my sides.

"Hang in there, Trip. I'll get you help if it's the last thing I do." And the way I feel, it will be.

I start down the sidewalk. I switch off suction. That way I can save a little power plus I avoid overfilling my waste bin.

Unlike the alley, this street has some light. The signs in some of the shop windows glow. Streetlamps illuminate the corners although they're too far away to do us any good. Beams from the headlights of passing cars break through the night.

Otherwise, it's dark. Clouds blanket the moon and stars. I hope they don't augur rain. If I have to, I can maneuver through small wet spots but with the extra weight I could get stuck in a puddle. I would, however, welcome another lightning zap. I'm running out of steam.

If he's anything like the Lady's cat, Trip won't like getting wet. The Lady gave Chloe a bath once. You would think the cat was being tortured. I could hear the yowling all the way across the cottage. Later I had to suck wet fur clumps and mop soapy water puddles off the bathroom floor.

The empty building housing the mega dealer is not in big demand. Not only does the Realtor's office lack customers, the shop window is dark. No one's inside holding down desks, manning phones, and drumming up business. It could be no one works at night.

The barber shop, the sculptor's studio, or whatever it is, and the café are more popular. Cars park next to the curb, people get out and dart into the shops. I hug the walls to avoid getting tramped on and hope not to attract the wrong attention.

"These stores are doing a lot of business," Trip says. "Maybe we should go the other way."

I can't tell what's beyond the self-storage building but dodging the pedestrians on this side of the street is filling me with anxiety. "I think you're right. Here we're likely to get crushed or kicked. I'll turn around and head the other way. We'll go as far as we need to see if we're likely to find help. If not, we'll cut through the alley and try the other street."

I reverse and retrace my path to the outlet. Staying on the asphalt, I skirt the curb and access the storage building's driveway. I'm making good progress when a car turns off the roadway and aims to park in front of a unit. I screech to a stop.

"What's wrong?" Trip asks. "Why aren't we moving."

"We almost got hit," I reply. I tuck us into the shadow cast by the cement block column separating the units. "We'll have to wait until they're done." And hope they don't take all day. Carrying a passenger is draining my power.

Despite the hour, the self-storage building is a busy place. With all the coming and going it takes what seems like hours to traverse the block. "I don't see much ahead that looks helpful, Trip. We should return to the alley." Especially since I'm weakening. I should at least deliver Trip to the location he's used to before I shut down.

"Wait! Can you see that?"

"See what?"

I feel Trip rearranging himself. "Can you see that sign? Way at the end of the sidewalk? Near the corner."

So far down the street as to be almost lost to view, a sign mounted on a rooftop eave flashes red and blue letters. I can't read but I can make out the image alongside the letters. In yellow it pictures the outlines of a cat and a dog. "Is that Animal Control? If it is, we want to avoid that."

"No, Eliot. I think that's a vet. I'll bet it's a vet."

"How can you tell? How do you know it's not Animal Control?"

"Because the animals in the picture are smiling. And there's a red cross."

He's right; the two animals are set against a background of a white cross with a red outline. In the TV shows, a red cross signifies a doctor, or at least emergency care.

"OK, Trip. We're on our way."

I've got one more storage unit to pass, then another shop before we're near what Trip thinks is a vet's clinic. I'm about to cross the asphalt when headlights from an approaching truck light the rollup door. I retreat into the shadows.

The truck comes to a stop. The truck door opens and the driver jumps out. He grabs a box from the truck bed. "You stay," he says, and approaches the keypad on the doorjamb. It reminds me of the system the Lady uses to secure the cottage's front door, at least when lightning hasn't fried the apparatus. Sure enough, after he presses a few keys, the door inches up.

"Hang on, Trip. We've got to wait out one more customer."

The door opens and the driver steps inside.

Then I hear a growl. If I had blood it would curdle. I risk a glance.

Chapter Sixteen

Leaning over the side of the truck's bed is the biggest, blackest, meanest canine I would ever hope to see. A labrador, Buster is a large dog but he's not hostile. Chloe's more vicious than he is.

This dog's eyes glint like the rocks in the alley's gutter. Its jowls hang almost to its broad chest. It draws back its lips, showing a row of teeth as sharp as the gang members' knives. Drool drips on the truck's side. Rising up, the dog plants huge paws on the truck bed rim. Its claws are long, sharp, and hooked. I see no collar around its thick neck. As far as I can tell it's not leashed or chained to the truck.

It narrows its glare at me.

No, not at me. At Trip.

If I had a heart it would pound.

Trip sees the dog too. I hear him gasp and feel him shimmy back, almost tipping me over.

He can't run. Well, he could, but not very fast, not with three legs and injured as well. There's nowhere to hide. We could duck into the storage unit but the dog would follow us, back us into a corner. My mop pads and brushes would be useless against him. A couple of swats with those huge paws and hooked claws and we'll be dead meat.

Do something, Eliot! *But what? What can I do?*

When confronted by the Lady's pets, I scoot under furniture where they can't reach me.

The Lady's pets ... that gives me an idea.

I shift into suction mode. With every bit of power I can summon I rev up and emit the loudest vacuum noise I can manage.

Trip whines in protest and that's not good but I can apologize later. And there will be a later because the dog whimpers. Wailing, it backs away from the truck bed rim and drops down. Its cries grow faint, in part muffled by the vehicle's sides and in part because the dog is cowering in a distant corner of the truck bed.

His owner exits the storage unit and keys the door closed. Returning to the truck, I hear him say, "Good dog." He reaches into the bed and his arm moves. I imagine he's patting the brute on the head. "We're done for tonight. Homeward bound and you get a treat for being a good doggie."

The truck backs down the drive and angles into a traffic lane. The dog peeks out over the tailgate but the vehicle is moving and he stays put. Good doggie. The red taillights grow faint as the truck and its lethal passenger disappear down the street.

If I had breath to hold, I'd be exhaling in relief.

We've got another shop to pass. Its darkened window suggests the store is closed. I can't tell from the items displayed what business is conducted there. The shop window frames an assortment of appliances: small ones like blenders, mixers, and food processors, all of which the Lady owns. In addition, I see larger appliances: an upright vacuum cleaner like Lux, a microwave oven, and a toaster.

"Not far to go now," I tell Trip, hoping we can make it to the vet before encountering any more threats. As I move forward, I notice we're leaving a thin trail on the pavement. Trip is dripping blood. He may have gotten "just" a flesh wound but it hasn't scabbed over.

"Yes, I think we're close," he replies. "I can see the sign clearly now."

"Close" is a matter of personal perspective. I'm so tired, I wonder if I can make it much farther. Skinny as he is, Trip is a noticeable weight. It takes all the power I've got to keep moving. I hope we can quit soon. The strain is depleting my batteries. The chances of finding a compatible docking station aren't little to none, they're zero to none. Sure, there could be a rogue lightning storm but I doubt it would do me any good without the intermediate power-supplying port.

Trip says, "The area seems familiar but it's hard to say. I always traveled in the carrier and never got a good look at my surroundings. It's been a while since I've been to the vet. Barb would bring me at least once a year, even if I wasn't sick. She called them wellness visits. Like I didn't know I was in for a lot of poking and prodding. A trip to the vet is never anything like fun. I don't like getting the shots and let's not even talk about the neutering. But he and Barb always treated me tenderly and I gotta say, kept me in good health."

"At least the street we've been on has been a lot nicer than the one where the alley is. You were right. That was one mean street."

"But it isn't anymore, Eliot."

"What are you saying? I never did get to clean—"

"Are you kidding? You mopped it up. You knocked down that dealer. You saved the police officer's life and he was able to make the arrest. That drugstore is out of business, for good. The school kids, the gang members, the hooker and the dirty cops, they won't be back." He sighs. "It's dark, Eliot."

Is Trip dying? Please, no, not after all we've been through. We've come so far. "Stay with me, Trip." It's what rescuers say on TV. "Don't die on me now."

Trip snorts. "What I mean is, we're here, we're at the vet. But the business is dark. The place isn't open. I didn't think it through but I guess it's not an emergency clinic."

"Well, can we hang out here until morning? Will you make it? Can you rest?"

"Rest? Are you kidding? I'm a cat. I can fall asleep in less time than it takes to say it. I don't remember when I last slept. I am way overdue for a nap."

"Sounds like a good idea. Conserve your strength. I'm sure we have only a few hours to wait."

"Ok. Hey, thanks for getting me this far. I couldn't have made it without you." Trip stretches out and drapes his legs over the sides of my lid. A moment later he's purring softly.

As for me, I couldn't go another inch. I'm sure the vet can tend to Trip's injuries but I'm done. Without my charger, I'm toast, not that the toaster in the shop next door could help.

But, I got the job done. I completed my assignment. I cleaned up the mean street. The city is safer. The boss will be proud of me. Maybe they'll hang my portrait in the station lobby with the other fallen officers.

As Trip said, it is dark. To save what power I've got left I've turned off my headlight. My motor winds down and stops. I shift into hibernation mode.

Until a brightening arouses me. It's morning, and a light has come on in the veterinary clinic.

I'm sapped. My collision sensors warn me about solid objects nearby and I will have to trust my instruments. I don't dare turn on my headlight or my motor.

I can hear, though. A lock clicks, a chime rings, and the door opens from inside.

Chapter Seventeen

"Well, would you look at this?" someone says.

Another voice says, "Oh, poor kitty. Do you think he crawled here on his own? How did he know he'd find a vet?"

The first voice, a man's, says, "Maybe someone dropped him off. Let's get him inside and look him over."

The second voice, a woman's says, "He's not dead, that's for sure. He's got a grip on—I don't know what this is. Some plastic object. Where did he find it? Did he drag it here or did someone leave it? Either way, he's got all his claws dug into the seams. He won't release it."

"Bring him in, plastic thingie and all. We can give him a little sedative. Then he might let go."

One of the people lifts me off the sidewalk. Trip hugs me tighter. His claws scratch my plastic housing but I don't mind; at least he's still alive.

I heard the vet say, "Joyce, I think it's Cuddles."

Cuddles? "I thought your name was Trip," I say to the cat.

"Cuddles was my home name." Whether he's speaking out loud or telepathically, his voice is weak and thin. "Trip is my street name."

"Cuddles was chipped," the vet says. Tall, with short dark hair and a clean-shaven face, he wears a white jacket buttoned over light-colored slacks. "Get the scanner, would you, and help me get him on the table." He carries us into an adjoining room. He spreads a sheet of white paper across a cabinet. A sink sits at one end, a scale on the other. The Lady has a gadget like it in her bathroom although I don't know why. Every time she stands on it, it makes her cranky.

The woman named Joyce slides a hand between Trip and me. Her nails are trimmed short and plain, unlike the Lady's which are long,

painted, and studded with tiny sparklers. Joyce lifts Trip off and sets
me on a counter in the entry room. The counter is crowded with bins
containing slips of paper with writing on them and bowls of tidbits.
Having vacuumed up similar items I recognize them as cat and dog treats.

A row of small armchairs bracketed by end tables line the wall
opposite the counter. Above them are mounted portraits of cats and
dogs. Maybe they're photos of patients, or they could be just friendly
furry faces. There are also printed pages, some bearing gold-colored
star-shaped stickers.

Though she also wears a white jacket and pale slacks, Joyce is shorter
than the vet and has fluffy blonde hair. She hustles to another room,
fetches a small orange plastic handheld device shaped a bit like a fat
magnifying glass and joins the other vet. He holds Trip steady on the
examining table and Joyce waves the device over the back of his neck.
"Yup, he's chipped."

"Can we get into the database to see who he is?"

"If you're certain it's Cuddles, I'll check the file."

One hand on Trip's shoulders, the vet strokes him with the other.

"Is this your vet, then?" I ask.

"Yes. He's a good guy."

"It's Cuddles, all right," Joyce reports.

"Great. Contact Mrs. Sanchez, then, and tell her we found her cat.
Tell her he's been injured but we're gonna fix him right up. Load me up
an anesthetic syringe and let's get him X-rayed."

"You're going to treat him now?"

"I gotta see what's going on with this wound."

"But you don't even have her authorization. What if she says 'no'?
Who's going to pay for it?"

"Hey, the little guy's in pain, I can see that. And if I'm going to treat
this injury, I need to do that now before infection sets in if it hasn't
already. I'll worry about the bill later."

Joyce sighs. "Free vaccination clinics. Discounts on spaying and neutering for the Humane Society. Tristan, how do you think this office is going to stay in business?"

"Oh, she'll authorize it. Four dogs and a cat—well, two cats now that she'll get Cuddles back. She's got a soft spot for animals."

"She's not the only one," Joyce mutters.

"Sounds like you'll be getting mended and going home," I say to Trip.

"Sounds like it."

He is tired and hurting, I can tell. His voice stream is feeble.

"Thanks for helping me."

"Don't mention it. You had my back."

"What's next for you? Are you going to tackle another crime?"

"That's what I do, Trip. I clean up the mean streets." Although at the moment, the street doesn't seem mean at all.

I sit on the counter and watch while Joyce and Tristan treat Trip. The anesthetic must be effective because I can no longer hear Trip's voice or thoughts.

"I don't know what gave him this scratch," Tristan says. "I don't think it's a claw mark from a fight. It's long and it singed his fur but it's not deep. Whoever dropped him off or however he got here, it wasn't a moment to soon. There's a little inflammation. Now that I've got the wound cleaned up, I can dress it and give him some antibiotic. That should prevent any opportunistic infection. Get him settled in the kennel, Joyce, let him sleep it off. We'll give him a complete checkup later when he's alert and we can test all his faculties. He's in pretty good shape, though, aside from being a little undernourished. Not much I can do about this older injury. The bones have already knitted. Little guy, you must have gotten into some kind of fight."

"Will you need to amputate that leg?"

"It's no good to him. He may be more comfortable without it. And the damaged tissue could lead to infection. I suspect surgery is the best option but I'll consult with Barb about it." Tristan collects his tools from his examination table and transfers them to the sink. If I could, I'd tell him I'd be happy to help clean. Not that the place needs my attention. It's almost antiseptic; the steel, aluminum, chrome, and shiny plastic surfaces gleam.

The chime at the door rings. Holding a paper cup in one hand and a bag in the other, a man enters. I don't think he's another vet. Instead of a white jacket, he wears pale blue coveralls. Hair tinged with gray tops a round, friendly face.

"Orville," says Tristan. "Starting work already?"

"In a minute. I've got a coffeemaker to fix that's giving me fits. The water pump doesn't work and I can't figure out why. Speaking of coffee, I stopped at that café for some java and donuts. Want one?"

"I'll never turn down a donut." Tristan reaches into the bag and withdraws a pastry.

Trip's nose twitches. I suspect he smells the donuts which I imagine have been part of his diet lately. He won't be sharing Tristan's bounty, though, because Joyce collects him from the examining table and carries him away.

"Hey, what you got here?" Orville pats my lid.

"I don't know. One of our patients brought it." Tristan chuckles.

"Ya know what this is? It's a robot vacuum cleaner."

"No kidding?"

"Does it work?"

"You tell me."

Orville presses my ON button. I try to respond but I'm depleted. "Hmm. This machine's got a problem. It could be clogged or need a filter change. Or it could simply be out of power. Did your patient leave you the charging station too?"

"No, only that unit."

"Mind if I take it? I'd like to tinker with it if you don't have plans for it."

"Be my guest."

Collecting his donut bag and tucking me under his arm, Orville exits the clinic.

Chapter Eighteen

Once inside the shop next door, Orville triggers the overhead lights. I can see that not only is the front window filled with appliances, so is the entire store. The variety of items is astounding. From small to large, the only thing they have in common that I can see is that they're all powered in some way, either by an electric cord or batteries. Lying partly disassembled on shelves or workbenches, they bear white tags with writing on them. Orville places me on a cluttered counter.

Now this shop could use a good clean. A deep clean. The few surfaces that aren't strewn with tagged devices are covered with dust.

Throughout the day people come into the shop. After a few customers, I gather that this is an appliance repair service. Some of the customers drop off items to be fixed. From the conversations, I gather the storm left quite a few devices on the fritz.

Others collect repaired equipment. The white tags identify to whom the broken items belong. Orville doesn't know about the Lady so I don't get a tag.

The light seeping through the hazy front window tells me it's midday. Orville takes a seat in a worn rolling task chair. He opens another paper sack and takes out a wrapped package. Removing the wrapper, he bites into one half of a sandwich. I wonder if it's tuna which makes me think of Trip. I hope the vet will feed him.

Orville narrows his eyes at me. Laying his sandwich aside, he picks me up. He turns my power switch off and then turns it on again. My motor emits a faint buzz.

"Hmm. Nothing wrong with the power switch. Let's see what else could be the trouble." He pops open my lid and lifts out my waste bin.

"Oh, my, you have been a busy beaver. This is stuffed. I'll bet you could hardly breathe."

He taps out the bin over a trash can and whisks the bin's mesh with a small paintbrush.

"And your filter, too," he says. He claps the filter against the trash can, then presses it into its recess in the waste bin and inserts the bin into its cavity. He flicks my power button on again but though I strain, I can't muster more than a low hum.

"Hmm," he says again. He leans back in his chair and frowns. "I know. I bet you're low on power. You need a recharge." He scratches his head, then slaps his temple. "And I think I've got the very thing." Orville stands and rummages in a roomy plastic tub tucked under a shelf. He returns, places a black, crescent-shaped box on the counter, and plugs its cord into a power strip. He then tucks me into the crescent.

Electricity surges into me. Thrilled, I blink my charging lights in gratitude.

Orville chortles. "They call me a pack rat but you know, ole buddy, it's a good thing I never throw anything away. Sometimes the little odd bit I tossed in a drawer is precisely what I need to get something working again." He pats me on my lid.

Comforted, I snuggle in for a power renewal.

Finishing his sandwich, Orville crumples the wrapper and tosses it into the trash can. He turns me off and unplugs the docking station. Slipping the both of us into his lunch sack, he flips a sign hanging on the door and exits the shop.

I hear another door chime.

"Orville," says Joyce. "Twice in one day. I see you've got another sack. Did you bring us more donuts?"

"No, but this is something I think you can use." He opens the sack and places me on the countertop next to the pet treats.

Across the room, Tristan looks over his shoulder. "Isn't that—?"

"The gadget you gave me this morning. It is. But I got it working. It's a Speckless—that's the brand name. Not only that, this model is especially good for cleaning up pet hair. Here, I'll show you." He sets me on the floor, switches me on, and presses the CLEAN button on my lid.

I don't waste a second but skate across the room, my brushes whirling. I don't know what Tristan and Joyce have been using but there's no way an upright or even a broom can get under some of those low shelves. I can, though. Let me at those furry tumbleweeds!

Orville says, "You'll want to do a little online research for this model. It needs a fresh filter. And a remote. With the remote, you can program it to clean even when you're not here. The filters aren't pricey and I doubt the remote is either. Cheaper than buying a whole outfit brand new.

"And if you want to get fancy, get the disposal dustbin. This vacuum has a self-emptying feature. But in the meantime, you can turn the cleaning off by pressing CLEAN again. Shut the whole thing down with the power button. And let it recharge with this." He takes the docking station from the paper bag. "You'll get a lot of use out of this device, won't you?"

Joyce says, "Oh, you bet. What a handy gadget."

Tristan says, "Isn't that something you could sell?"

Orville scoffs. "Not without the remote. But for your purposes, it should do fine even without it."

"Well, I ... well. Donuts and a vacuum cleaner. This is my lucky day."

"OK, back to work." With a thumbs up, Orville leaves the clinic.

Customers arrive to drop off or pick up pet patients. The owners are curious about Tristan's robot cleaner but dogs on leashes and cats in carriers balk at the sound of my vacuum.

"We'd better put this aside for the time being," Joyce says. She pauses my cleaning and powers me down. She wedges the docking station into a corner under a guest chair and puts me in place.

I sit contentedly on my docking station, soaking up power and watching TV. Mounted on the wall, it entertains people while they wait.

It broadcasts much of the same fare the Lady would watch: newscasts, talk programs, game shows.

A movie comes on and I hear a voice I recognize.

"You did good, Eliot."

It's the Boss. He's behind his desk only instead of leaning on it he's seated behind it, his hands folded on the blotter. His face is far more relaxed than when I last saw him.

"I'll be recommending you for a commendation," the boss says. "I know when I first gave you the assignment you had your doubts but I knew you could do it."

I did have my doubts, I want to tell him. There were moments when I was ready to give up. But you were counting on me, Boss. The city was counting on me. Even Trip was counting on me at the end.

"I'm giving you a new charge. I'm putting you on non-enforcement duty for the time being," the boss says. "I can see this last assignment took its toll. You need a chance to catch your breath, and regain your strength."

Chapter Nineteen

Indeed, I do, Boss. Cleaning the mean street and rescuing Trip depleted every ounce of energy I had. Orville emptying my waste bin and flushing my filter did me a world of good. I can suction once again. And while getting galvanized by lightning was electrifying, pun intended, the slow and steady flow of power from this docking station is more my speed.

The chime sounds and a woman comes through the door. She's not a vet either; she wears a sweater and jeans. Long curly black hair flows to her shoulders. One hand is wrapped around the handle of a cat carrier. The other is gripped by a little boy. His dark hair, though short, is curly like his mom's. He wears a long-sleeved tee shirt and coveralls embroidered with the outlines of puppies and kittens.

The woman places the carrier on the floor. I can see it's empty so she's not dropping off a patient, she's picking one up.

"Barb!" Joyce cries.

Oh, she's here for Trip.

"I'll go get Cuddles." Joyce vanishes into the other room and returns with Trip.

"Cuddles," cries the little boy. He scurries to Joyce and holds out his arms.

Joyce hands him Trip.

The little boy holds him close to his chest.

"Now, don't squeeze him too hard, Honey," the woman says. "He's got an ow-ie. You don't want to make him feel worse."

Trip stretches up and butts the boy's chin with the top of his head.

"Mama, can I give him a treat?" the boy asks.

The woman gives Joyce a questioning look. Joyce nods.

"Just one, OK? Here, give Cuddles to me and you go get him a snack."

The woman takes Trip from her son. He toddles to the counter, stands on tiptoe, and snatches a morsel from one of the dishes. He holds it out to Trip who sniffs it, catches it with the tip of his tongue, and crunches it.

Barb brushes her hand down Trip's back and he purrs.

"Poor baby," she says. "Where have you been? Look at you, you're so skinny. I can't wait to get you home and get you fattened up."

I hear Trip say, "I can't wait either. Cheezy-Ohs were fine but I miss those little cans of tuna paté."

Barb says, "And what happened to your leg?"

Joyce replies, "We can talk about that. We don't see any signs of infection but we want to give it a closer look."

Barb piles Trip into the carrier and leans on the counter. "What do I owe you?" she asks.

Joyce says, "I'll get you an invoice. And a printout of the therapy he got. Plus, we want him to stay on a course of antibiotics so I'll give you instructions about that too. We'd like to examine him again in a week. We can talk about his leg, then, too."

Trips says, "Eliot, I see you've got a docking station."

"Yeah. Orville who has the appliance repair shop next door found it. Now that I'm all powered up, Tristan and Joyce are going to keep me so I can clean the clinic."

"Wow, that sounds like a much better assignment than mopping up that alley. I'm sure not going to miss it and I'll bet neither will you."

"I'm gonna miss you, though, Trip." I didn't realize how much I would until I said it.

"I'll miss you, too, Eliot. But this isn't goodbye. This is just goodbye for now. Barb will bring me back for that checkup, and at least once a year for a wellness visit and updates on my shots. I won't mind the injections so much now that I know I'll get to visit with you."

Barb picks up the carrier and heads for the door.

"Be seein' ya, Eliot," Trip says as they exit the clinic.

"Be seein' ya, Trip."

Trip's right. I'll miss hanging with him but I don't miss that alley at all. The warm feeling I've got isn't solely from the power seeping in from the docking station. It's also the satisfaction of a job well done.

Caring for patients and their owners keeps Tristan and Joyce busy. I hear the patients' communication. Not speech so much, more like cries of pain and fear. I don't talk to them. An unfamiliar disembodied voice could upset them even more. I send out waves of compassion, of sympathy, comfort, and reassurance that Tristan and Joyce are caring, competent people. The animals settle down even before their sedative kicks in so I think I'm doing some good.

The front window frames a darkening sky. The day is coming to an end.

Joyce turns off the TV, strides to the front door, and locks it.

She and Tristan start for the rear of the clinic.

She switches off the overhead lights. "Hold on a sec," Joyce says. She bends down and peeks under the chair. "Yup. Still charging." Straightening, she says, "I'll spend time tonight on a search engine hunting up that remote. Can you imagine? We can program the cleaner to work overnight, come in to work in the morning and find the place spic and span. Won't that be cool, Tristan?" She chuckles. "Did you notice? It's got a big S on its lid."

"That's the brand name," Tristan says. "Orville said it stands for Speckless."

"I think it stands for Sunday. Which I get back now that I don't have to come in and vacuum the clinic. Or, even better: Stupendous. Yeah, that's what that S stands for. Stupendous."

Stupendous. I like that much better than Stupid.

"Yup," says Joyce, "this was our lucky day, Tristan."

Mine too, nice Lady. Mine too.

Also by Devorah Fox

The Bewildering Adventures of King Bewilliam series:

The Lost King, Book One

The King's Ransom, Book Two

The King's Redress, Book Three

The Redoubt, Book Four

Naked Came the Sharks with Jed Donellie

Murder by the Book, A Mystery Mini ebook

One Bad Apple, A Mystery Mini ebook

Detour

The Zen Detective

The *Lady Blackwing* ebook series

Lady Blackwing

Lady Blackwing Gets Her Moniker

Lady Blackwing Earns Her Mask

Lady Blackwing Screws Up

Lady Blackwing Battles the Master of the Keys

Don't miss out!

Visit the website below and you can sign up to receive emails whenever Devorah Fox publishes a new book. There's no charge and no obligation.

https://books2read.com/r/B-A-NXEH-NWAAF

BOOKS 2 READ

Connecting independent readers to independent writers.

Did you love *Speckless and the Mean Streets*? Then you should read *Lady Blackwing, A Struggling Superhero Fantasy/Science Fiction Mini*[1] by Devorah Fox!

Mercedes is just trying to make her way through life: taking classes, working her shift as a barista, and writing short stories that she never seems to finish. After a minor accident, she finds herself imbued with startling powers. She projects future events and rewrites the past, with disastrous consequences. Her first attempts to use her strange talents incite a zombie attack and bring an Egyptian goddess to life. Stunned by awesome abilities that she can't seem to control, Mercedes wonders if she's been cursed. Can she be cured? And if she can't, what then?

Read more at www.devorahfox.com.

---

1. https://books2read.com/u/br11eW

2. https://books2read.com/u/br11eW

About the Author

It's said of Devorah Fox that she writes outside the box. Its feelings hurt, the box gets up and stomps off. So she writes about that, too.

A multi-genre author, she has written a best-selling epic fantasy series, "The Bewildering Adventures of King Bewilliam," as well as an acclaimed mystery and a popular thriller, and co-authored a contemporary thriller with Jed Donellie. She contributed short stories to a variety of anthologies, penned several Mystery and Fantasy Short Reads, and has several five-star ghostwriting projects to her name. Born in Brooklyn, New York, she now lives on the Texas Gulf Coast with rescued tabby cats ... and a dragon named Inky.

Read more at www.devorahfox.com.